For my family
—K.A.

To my parents for
encouraging my love for art
—M.

Faith Takes the Train
Text copyright © 2025 by Kesi Augustine
Illustrations copyright © 2025 by Mokshini
All rights reserved. Manufactured in Capriate San Gervasio, Italy.
No part of this book may be used or reproduced in any manner whatsoever without written permission
except in the case of brief quotations embodied in critical articles and reviews. For information address
HarperCollins Children's Books, a division of HarperCollins Publishers, 195 Broadway, New York, NY 10007.
www.harpercollinschildrens.com

Library of Congress Control Number: 2024944602
ISBN 978-0-06-325134-2

The artist used acrylic paint and watercolor with digital touchups to create the illustrations for this book.
Typography by Dana Fritts
24 25 26 27 28 RTLO 10 9 8 7 6 5 4 3 2 1

First Edition

Faith Takes the Train

written by
KESI AUGUSTINE

illustrated by
MOKSHINI

HARPER
An Imprint of HarperCollinsPublishers

It's the same old train ride home from Grandma's house.
We're squished in our seats.
Everyone is talking.
The train twists and turns.

Mama lets me munch on a peanut-butter-and-jelly sandwich.
"Just one bite," Mama says.
The sandwich is gooey with honey from Grandma's beehive.

Mmm. Delicious!
I shimmy while I eat.

Suddenly, I hear: *Ahem, ahem!*
It's Isaiah! Our old neighbor.
He sings to us every day.
But today, Isaiah shouts, "Good evening!
My son and I have fallen on hard times."

"Could anyone please spare some change?" Isaiah asks.

Silence swallows the train.

"A bite to eat?"

Nobody looks.

"Well," Isaiah says, "thank you for your time."

Does anyone care?

Isaiah looks at me.
Peanut butter sticks to my teeth.
I see his face. I hear his words.
My heart *thump-thump-thump*s.

I open my lunch box.
I find one last piece of my sandwich.
Mama holds my hand. "Be mindful," she says.
"Would you like a snack?" I whisper to Isaiah.
"Thank you," Isaiah replies. "*Mmm.* Peanut butter and jelly . . . with honey! *De*licious."

"Thank you, . . ."
"Faith," I say.
Isaiah smiles. "Bless you, Faith!"

The train twists and turns.
Everyone talks again.
"How sweet of you," Mama says.
My heart *thump-thump-thump*s.
Isaiah walks away.
I say a silent goodbye.

Someone is playing a keyboard at our stop.

Do-be-do-be . . . *bum bum.*

Its sound fills the tunnel.

I wonder, *Does Isaiah like grape jelly?*
Or marvelous mint?
Does he like smooth peanut butter?
Or one with a crunch?

I wonder more and more . . .

Does Isaiah's son like sandwiches too?
Maybe we could take the train to our house . . .
make a bunch of gooey sandwiches . . .
and have a feast!

and shimmy to Isaiah's songs.

A new train twists and turns into the station. *Screeeeech!*
The musician takes a bow.
People clap their hands.

A little girl smiles at me through the train window.
I smile back.
I feel a *thump-thump-thump*.
Tomorrow, another train will come.
Will I see Isaiah again?

"Can we bring an extra sandwich tomorrow?" I ask Mama.
"Mmm," Mama replies. "That is a *de*licious idea."

And we walk along the platform, journeying home...

. . . with hearts full of faith.

AUTHOR'S NOTE

Dear Reader,

In 2020 COVID-19 changed our world. Many people lost their homes. Many people lost their jobs. Many people needed food. Yet the government did not give enough support to everyone.

Ordinary people came together.

"Everyone has something to offer, and everyone has something they need," an organization in Sunnyside, Queens, explained. This is called mutual aid, and it's a way we can help our neighbors in need.

Mutual aid can look like helping neighbors and elders to get their groceries and medicine, planting community gardens, starting soup kitchens, filling a community fridge, and so much more. I volunteered with neighbors in Woodside, Queens. We filled a local fridge with food. Anyone could give or take food. Today there are over one hundred sixty fridges in New York City.

Soon the city reopened. I took the train to work every day. I noticed more and more neighbors in need. Some slept on the train. Others lived in train stations. I felt sad, wondering what I could possibly do.

I read about our houseless neighbors—how this wasn't a new problem in our community, but how it was increasingly getting worse. And how hunger can affect everyone, no matter their housing status.

Suddenly, I felt inspired to write a story about care. Faith's story happens on the train because sometimes the neighbors who need our help are seated right beside us. When I met Isaiah, I heard him singing, like many travelers often do. Isaiah experiences hunger and is on the verge of houselessness, and he uses his voice to help him through tough times. I hope Isaiah seems familiar to us. Someone real.

Faith connects with Isaiah and imagines what it would be like to have a feast. But how we feed each other requires responsibility and caution. Unfortunately, in many cities, feeding people in public spaces is criminalized. But there is still room for someone to open their heart and make a gesture to prove that there are people who care whether another human being has something to eat. Faith is that someone, and we can be too.

What if we lived in a world where we nourished everyone with love, sweetness, and dignity? Let's imagine together that our life is one long train ride. There's a seat on this train especially for you. How will you show your care to other passengers? Let a little imagination and heartful of faith fuel your journey.

Love,
Kesi

RESOURCES

If you want to offer help to neighbors in need, here are just a few resources to consider:

UNHOUSED NEIGHBORS
- Coalition for the Homeless: www.coalitionforthehomeless.com
- Sesame Street Workshop—Homelessness: www.sesame-workshop.org/topics/homelessness

HUNGER
- Feeding America: Find Your Local Soup Kitchen: www.feedingamerica.org
- Feed Black Futures: www.feedblackfutures.org
- Hannah's Hope Houses: www.hhhouses.org (Hannah began helping at age ten!)
- Holy Apostles Soup Kitchen: www.holyapostlesnyc.org
- Miriam's Kitchen: www.miriamskitchen.org

MUTUAL AID
- Big Door Brigade: www.bigdoorbrigade.com/what-is-mutual-aid
- Mutual Aid Hub: www.mutualaidhub.org
- Centro Corona Mutual Aid: bit.ly/CentroMutualAid
- Sunnyside & Woodside Mutual Aid: www.swma.nyc

COMMUNITY FRIDGES
- NYC Community Fridge Map: nycfridge.com
- Find a Community Fridge in Your Local Community: www.changex.org/us/communityfridge/locations
- Start a Community Fridge: www.fridgefinder.app/pamphlet/get-involved/start-a-fridge

FURTHER READINGS

Bunting, Eve. *Fly Away Home*. New York: Clarion Books, 1991.

de la Peña, Matt. *Last Stop on Market Street*. New York: G.P. Putnam's Sons, 2015.

Du Bois, W. E. B. *The Brownies' Book*. 1920–1921.

Mora, Oge. *Thank You, Omu!* New York: Little, Brown and Company, 2018.

Nagara, Innosanto. *A Is for Activist*. New York: Triangle Square, 2013.

Reading Rainbow Stories, "Fly Away Home." Aired 1996 on PBS. www.thinktv.pbslearningmedia.org/resource/fly-away-home-video/reading-rainbow-stories.